CHRISTMAS IN THE CITY

STORY AND PICTURES BY

Loretta Krupinski

HYPERION BOOKS FOR CHILDREN

NEW YORK

For information address Hyperion Books for Children,

114 Fifth Avenue, New York, New York 10011-5690.

Designed by Christine Kettner

First Edition

1 3 5 7 9 10 8 6 4 2

Printed in Hong Kong

Library of Congress-Cataloging-in-Publication data on file.

ISBN 0-7868-0834-9 (tr.) ISBN 0-7868-2652-5 (lib. ed.)

Visit www.hyperionchildrensbooks.com

To BILL—who kept my spirit and
me warm on a very cold day
at Rockefeller Center

NEW YORK CITY was preparing for Christmas. People rushed up and down the sidewalks from one corner to the next, carrying packages and gifts. Windows were decorated, wreaths were hung, and little twinkling lights were wrapped around the bare branches of trees, which glowed at night like blossoms.

The tree rose tall and proud in Rockefeller Plaza. Eight thousand lights sparkled like jewels from the top of the tree to the bottom. Christmas balls the size of grapefruit hung from its branches.

Then, when the saws stopped buzzing, the car horns stopped honking, and the workmen's voices finally fell silent, two tiny mice peeked out from a hole in the tree's trunk.

"My dear, our home has now become a Christmas tree," said Mr. Mouse.

"The biggest one of all!" said Mrs. Mouse.

Hundreds of people looked back up at the tree, while the mice watched the skaters below. They were country mice. The tree was their home. Now they found themselves at Rockefeller Center in the heart of New York City.

After they had tidied up the furniture and gathered up the spilled seeds, Mrs. Mouse said, "Let's explore! I want to see *everything!*"

"Are you certain you're up to it?" asked Mr. Mouse.

Mrs. Mouse was expecting babies.

"You never know when the little ones will arrive," said Mrs. Mouse. "But now we're here in a big city. Come with me!"

With the slim crescent moon gleaming in the sky, the two mice walked hand in hand down the now dark and deserted sidewalk.

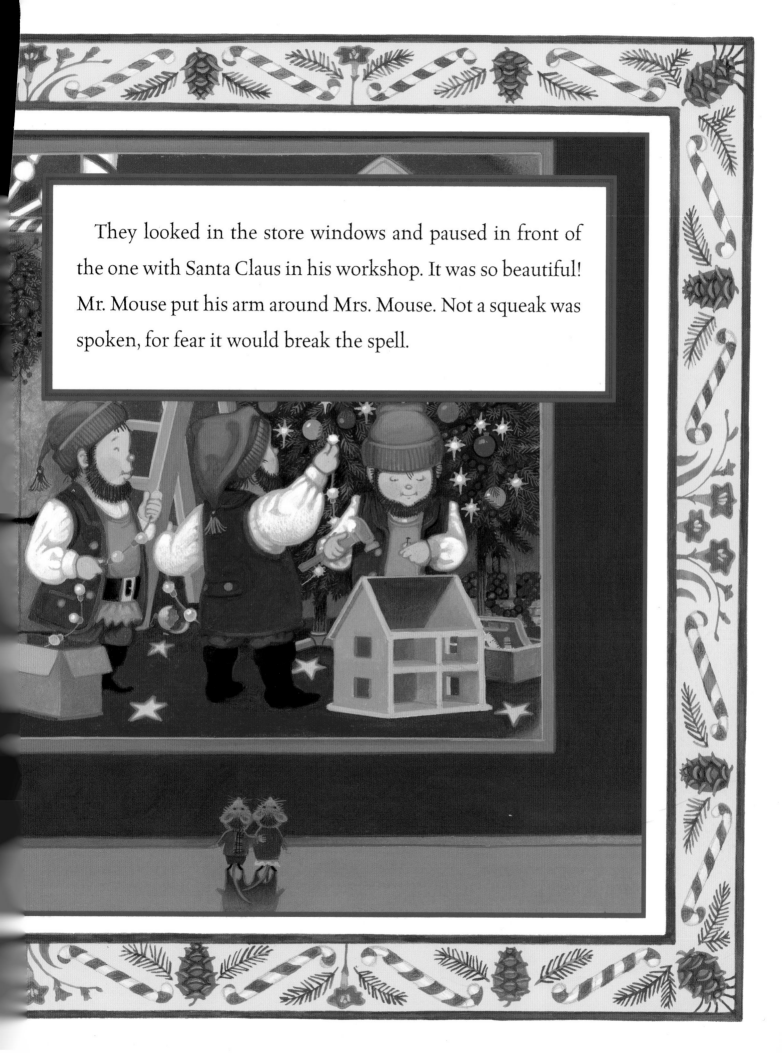

They looked in the store windows and paused in front of the one with Santa Claus in his workshop. It was so beautiful! Mr. Mouse put his arm around Mrs. Mouse. Not a squeak was spoken, for fear it would break the spell.

The next night, Mrs. Mouse spotted a toy store.

"Wouldn't it be wonderful to live in a dollhouse like that instead of in a tree?" she sighed.

"Good idea, Mrs. Mouse. We could use one of the rooms to store seeds and nuts," said Mr. Mouse.

"And I could have a nursery for our babies," she added.

On the way home, they found part of a pretzel and an apple core.

"Here, stuff the apple seeds in your pockets," Mr. Mouse said, "and I'll carry this piece of bread. I'll race you across the ice rink, back to the tree."

They skimmed across the ice like two feathers being blown by the wind.

By day they slept and dreamed. At night, the rosy glow
from the Christmas lights filled their home. They dined on
seeds and planned their walks.

"Tonight," said Mr. Mouse, "let's see what's at the bottom
of those stairs that go underground."

"Oh, yes!" said Mrs. Mouse. "Maybe we'll find some
mouse friends."

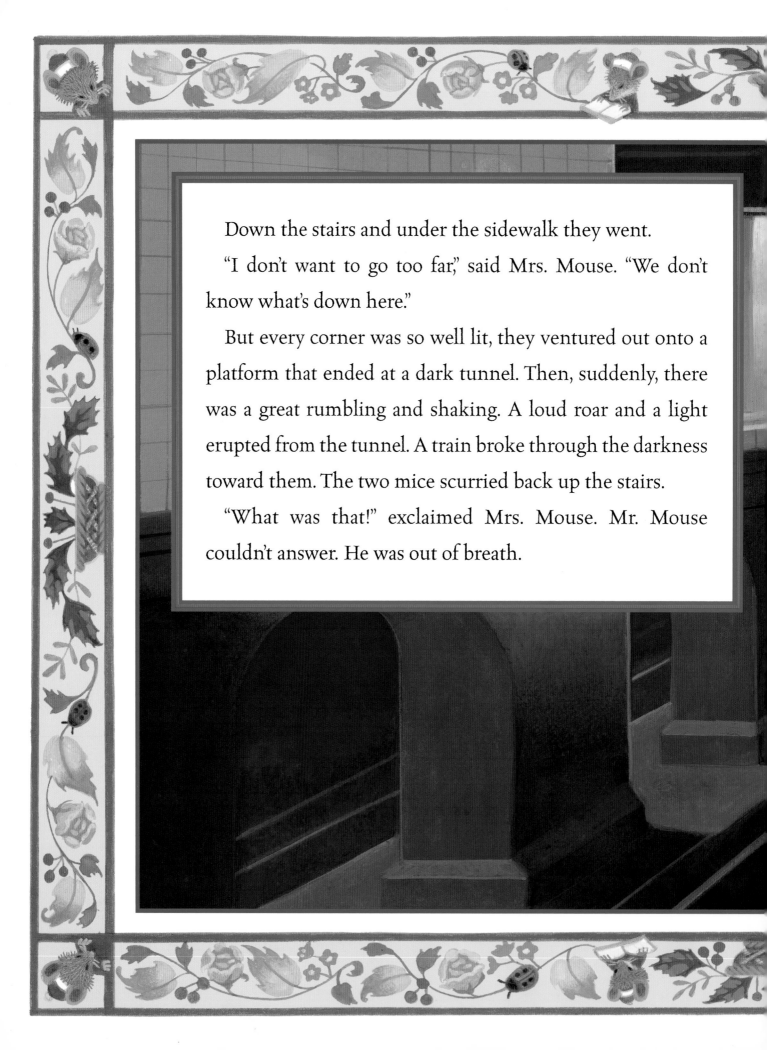

Down the stairs and under the sidewalk they went.

"I don't want to go too far," said Mrs. Mouse. "We don't know what's down here."

But every corner was so well lit, they ventured out onto a platform that ended at a dark tunnel. Then, suddenly, there was a great rumbling and shaking. A loud roar and a light erupted from the tunnel. A train broke through the darkness toward them. The two mice scurried back up the stairs.

"What was that!" exclaimed Mrs. Mouse. Mr. Mouse couldn't answer. He was out of breath.

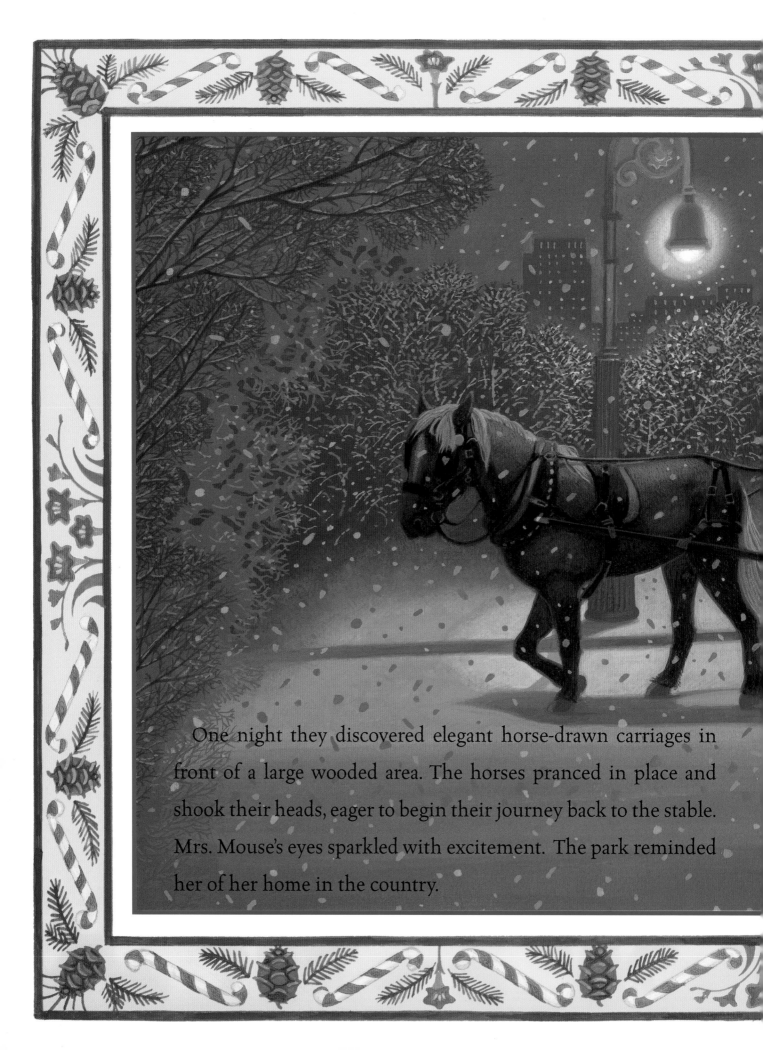

One night they discovered elegant horse-drawn carriages in front of a large wooded area. The horses pranced in place and shook their heads, eager to begin their journey back to the stable. Mrs. Mouse's eyes sparkled with excitement. The park reminded her of her home in the country.

"Oh, could we look for a new tree? When the babies arrive, I want them to live here, where there are plenty of trees and grass."

"Good idea, Mrs. Mouse. First, let's hitch a ride on a carriage," said Mr. Mouse. As they did, snowflakes the size of mouse ears began to fall.

On their next stroll, between two buildings they saw a great star swinging among the real stars in the midnight sky. Hundreds of little white lights twinkled as it swayed in the gentle evening breeze. The star led them to a building with a tall steeple, adorned with a cross on top. The stone exterior was carved as delicately as lace.

"I think we should go in here," said Mrs. Mouse. "The babies are coming. We don't have time to get back to the tree."

The door was open enough for small mice to enter. Inside, the glow of a thousand candles filled the room.

"Let's not go in there, dear. Too many people," said Mr.
Mouse. He remembered a manger scene in the churchyard.

"Come with me. I know where to go," he said.

He led Mrs. Mouse to the soft bed of straw. She laid her
head against his chest, and he pulled the straw over them.
Then he wrapped his arms around her, peeking at the real
star that winked overhead.

That night, three baby mice were born
in the churchyard.

"Merry Christmas," said a small dog to the mice. "Don't be afraid. Don't you know tonight is Christmas Eve? That means there is peace and goodwill between all animals. I've brought you a present," he said, dropping half a doughnut onto the straw.

Later that same evening, a squirrel perched on the manger above the mice. "Merry Christmas," he said, after dropping a peanut he was holding.
"It's for you."

A striped cat was attracted to the movement in the straw.

"Do not be afraid," she said to the mice. "I come with peace in my heart and a chestnut for you."

That Christmas Eve, Mr. and Mrs. Mouse were truly blessed.
They were surrounded by love, comfort—and their new babies.

The very next evening, Mr. and Mrs. Mouse bundled up the babies against the cold and, creeping cautiously, hurried back to their home in Rockefeller Center. The warmth from the rosy glow of the Christmas lights spread through their little home. Cozy days and nights came and went as they took care of their new family.

Then, one morning, peace and harmony came to an end. They peeked out to see the workmen untangling the long strands of lights. Christmas balls were unhooked. As happens to Christmas trees, this one was coming down.

"What do we do now?" exclaimed Mrs. Mouse.

"It's too late to climb down the tree, dear. Just hang on!" called Mr. Mouse. As the mouse family firmly clutched their babies, the tree was neatly laid onto the flatbed truck.

Through the city they went, as the car horns beeped and the gears on the truck grumbled, shifted, and purred.

Soon they were back in the countryside where they had come from.

The little field mice left their tree that day and searched for a new home. They came across an old barn. Up in the rafters, amid old chairs and trunks, and much to Mrs. Mouse's delight, they found a dollhouse. They filled one room with seeds and nuts, and another room with the babies.

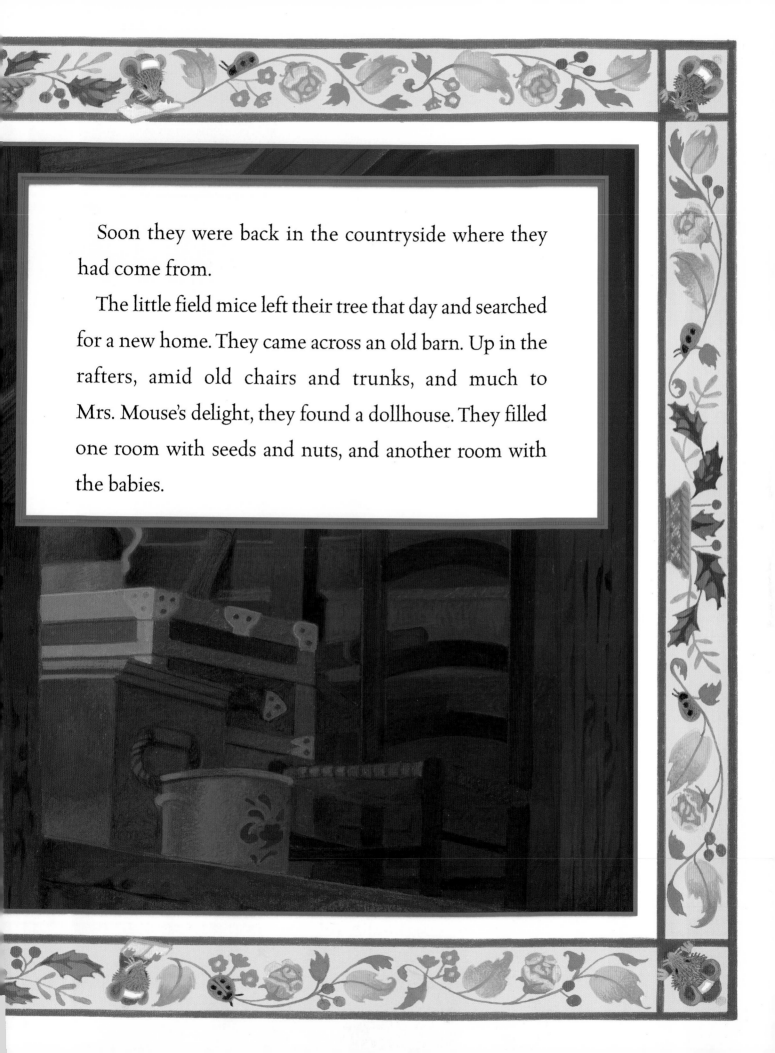